Speak To The Sickness & Disease!!!

By

Scott Jay Daniels

Dedication

Table of Contents

Dedication iii

Acknowledgments v

Chapter 1 The Divine Encounter 1

Chapter 2 The Revelation of Healing 2

Chapter 3 Faith vs Religion 4

Chapter 4 God's Healing Nature 6

Chapter 5 Authority Over Sickness 8

Chapter 6 Speaking to the Mountain 10

Chapter 7 Walking in Divine Health 12

Chapter 8 What Hinders Healing? 14

Chapter 9 Religion vs Relationship 16

Chapter 10 Teaching the Next Generation 18

Chapter 11 Practical Declarations and Daily Practices 19

Chapter 12 Scriptures for Healing and Authority 25

Chapter 13 Scriptural Methods of Healing 27

Conclusion 29

Acknowledgments

Chapter 1
The Divine Encounter

In the fall of 2020, I was touched deeply by the power of God. Touched deeply by the Holy Spirit in a way I had never known before. Laughter, joy, and peace flooded my soul. I was not gasping for breath or overwhelmed with human emotion—this was supernatural joy. I was laughing hysterically, yet breathing like I was at complete rest. This was holy. It was heavenly.

That moment changed me. It wasn't an emotional high or a momentary inspiration. It was the beginning of a journey into God's Word and into a deeper understanding of who Jesus is, not just as Savior, but as Healer.

I started traveling, making trips to the River Church in Tampa, Florida, to sit under the teaching of Pastor Rodney Howard-Browne. Along the way, I would listen to testimonies and sermons from other ministers I heard spoken about at the River Church. I became especially captivated by the life and healing testimony of Kenneth Hagin. I literally would spend hours listening to and searching the Scriptures on what I heard from Kenneth Hagin. I would often play these messages over and over, discovering new truth about God and His Word that I never realized or heard taught before. I devoured his messages, listening until I practically could preach the same message. Lol. These messages stirred God's truth—God's very Word—in me. I knew God was speaking to me, and I would never go back to life as usual.

Chapter 2
The Revelation of Healing

As I listened to these men of faith, the Holy Spirit began to show me truth after truth. I was confronted with the radical idea that no born-again believer needs to be sick or deal with any diseases.

Now, I know that sounds foreign, and even crazy, especially to Christians who have lost loved ones or battled illness themselves. My own family has a history of loss from cancer, heart disease, and other illnesses. So, when I began to share these Biblical truths about divine healing, they were not as well received as I expected. I would even say they went over like a lead balloon. Lol. Some of my closest family strongly disagreed with my findings.

But I could not deny what I was experiencing and what God was revealing to me through His Word. This was not my opinion. This was God's Word, God's Truth.

I believed others would be as excited to hear this good news as I was. I even shared about healing on Facebook posts, confident that other believers in Christ would celebrate these truths. I was wrong, and the backlash was real. This was a good lesson for me because it revealed something I did not know before: people know Jesus as Savior, but not Jesus as their Healer.

That realization only intensified my mission. I had to get this truth to the world. Healing is already ours! We only need to believe it, speak it, and walk in it, praising Jesus for it, because it was provided 2,000 years ago when Jesus took those stripes on His back at Calvary.

Chapter 3
Faith vs Religion

"All Sickness and Disease Come from Satan—Not from God!"

That was one of my first public declarations, and it set off a firestorm. Why? Because many Christians have been religiously taught that God uses sickness and disease to teach His children lessons. That is not just wrong, but it's dangerously wrong! They don't realize that, in complete ignorance, they are accusing God of child abuse.

God teaches us through His Word, not through suffering and harm. Sickness and disease have one purpose, and that is to harm us and ultimately kill us. Jesus showed us the heart of the Father when He healed everyone who came to Him for healing. Not once did Jesus turn away anyone who came to Him for healing. The religious spirit will say, "Maybe God is trying to teach me something through this illness." God's Word doesn't say that! Jesus healed the sick and set free the oppressed. Jesus said He only does what the Father is doing **(John 5:19).**

So, what do we see Jesus doing? He heals, delivers, and sets the captive free! That means the Father's will is to heal, deliver, and set the captives free! The Bible says that in the presence of God is fullness of joy!

"

Religion clouds the view of God as Healer and paints Him as this angry, spiteful Father who hurts His kids to teach them lessons, a God who picks and chooses whom He feels deserves healing. That's not what the Bible teaches us at all. God's Word teaches us that God is a loving God and that all good and perfect gifts come from God. God is loving and does not want anyone to perish or be lost. It's the goodness of God that leads us to salvation. God wants us all healed and walking in divine health, just like He wants us all saved. His Son Jesus provided this for us, but we have to believe it and receive it.

God's Word teaches us the truth. It's by faith we are saved. It's by faith we are healed, and it's by faith we see God as our Father who restores us. It's by faith we see Jesus as our Savior who bore our sickness and disease so we don't have to **(Isaiah 53:5 & Matthew 8:17).**

Chapter 4
God's Healing Nature

God's name is Jehovah Rapha – "The Lord who heals you" **(Exodus 15:26).** Healing isn't just something God does; healing is who God is. We find this truth in the Word.

Scripture after scripture confirms this:

Psalms 103:3 – "who forgives all your iniquities and heals all your diseases."

Jeremiah 30:17 – "I will restore health to you, and your wounds I will heal, declares the Lord."

1 Peter 2:24 – "by His stripes we were healed."

Jesus taught these truths in the New Testament. He healed all who were sick **(Matthew 8:16).** He said the works that He did, we will do, and even greater works than these **(John 14:12).** Jesus gave us authority (power) over all the power of the enemy **(Luke 10:19).**

Why then are so many in the Church sick and diseased?

Because they don't know and haven't been taught what is already theirs, already provided to them by Jesus at Calvary. They choose to believe the doctor's report over what the Bible says. They put more faith in the doctors than they do in God and His Word. But healing has already been provided by God through Jesus Christ, and it is a completed work.

We don't need to beg God for healing – pleading to be healed like the leper **(Mark 1:40).** We just need to activate our faith and believe what God's Word says is true!

Chapter 5
Authority Over Sickness

Jesus didn't leave us powerless. Jesus tells us in His Name:

"You lay hands on the sick, and they will recover." **(Mark 16:18)**

"Whatever you say, believing and not doubting, you will have. Speak to the mountain…and it will move." **(Mark 11:23)**

"You have authority over the enemy!" **(Luke 10:19)**

Sickness and disease are mountains sent by the enemy to attack your body. Jesus told us to speak to the mountain. Don't ignore it, don't deny it, but command it to leave in Jesus' Name!

Do you believe in God? Do you believe God's Word is true? Then you have everything you need to activate your faith by speaking to the mountain and telling it to go now, in Jesus' Name!

This is how I live my life now. The first symptom of an attack, I don't panic or get anxious. I don't run to the medicine cabinet. I open my mouth and speak the Word of God.

I say out loud:

"I am healed and whole by His stripes. Jesus took those stripes on His back at Calvary for my healing, and I receive the healing He provided and walk in divine health, completely healed and made whole, in Jesus' Name!"

I command all symptoms of sickness, illness, disease, and allergies to go in the mighty name of Jesus Christ! Then I praise Jesus and thank God for my healing, before it is even manifested. Because I know God's Word is true, and I am healed by His Name and faith in His Name, regardless of how I feel at that time. That is how we activate our faith, by the words we speak!

Chapter 6
Speaking to the Mountain

Jesus said something very radical in Mark 11:23:

"Whoever says to this mountain, 'Be removed and be cast into the sea,' and does not doubt in his heart, but believes that those things he says will be done, he will have whatever he says."

Notice, Jesus didn't say, "Pray about the mountain," or "Ask God to move the mountain for you." He said, **"Speak to it."**

This changes everything.

Most believers talk to God about their problems. They ask Him to deal with the situation and remove it. But Jesus said to **speak to the problem**, in **His name** and with **His authority**. That's powerful!

That's exactly what I do every time a symptom tries to attack my body. I speak to it directly, with boldness and authority in Christ Jesus!

Example (Spoken Out Loud):

"Headache, you leave my body now, in Jesus' name! I've been redeemed by the blood of Jesus Christ and given authority by God through Him. I command all symptoms of sickness, illness, or disease to leave my body now, in Jesus' name. By His stripes I am healed and whole. I walk in divine health, completely healed by Jesus Christ. Any unclean spirit or spirit of infirmity, go now from me, in Jesus' name, and do not come back, in the mighty name of Jesus Christ!"

Follow up with praise:

Praising God, my Father, thanking and praising Jesus for the healing He provided for me at Calvary, and thanking the Holy Spirit for giving life to every part of my body!

The **Word of God**, spoken in **faith through our mouths**, is one of the most powerful weapons we have as born-again believers. Never forget, **God moves mightily to perform His Word.** The Bible tells us that **God watches over His Word to perform it** (Jeremiah 1:12).

Chapter 7
Walking in Divine Health

The Difference Between Being Healed and Walking in Divine Health

Healing means something attacked your body, but you recovered, and you were made whole.

Divine health, on the other hand, means you live above sickness, illness, and disease. You resist any attack before it even has a chance to manifest.

God has provided both healing and divine health through Jesus Christ and the indwelling of the Holy Spirit. The key is to stay full of God's Word and His Spirit!

You don't wait for symptoms to appear. Instead, you immerse yourself in the Word of God, renewing your mind, filling your heart with His truth, and worshiping in His presence. You live in a constant state of awareness of God's presence and His hand upon you.

Speak God's Word aloud, thank Him for His promises, His blessings, and His mercies, which truly are new every morning! Renew your mind daily through His Word and in prayer. Ask Him to reveal Himself to you, to give you revelation knowledge of who He is and what His Word says. It's a relationship with Him, one filled with promises revealed in those who believe.

So, when the enemy tries to attack, you don't flinch. You declare with authority:

"Sickness, illness, disease, or any infirmity, you die before you even touch my body, in Jesus' name! You have no right to even try to attack me! You are a defeated foe, defeated by Jesus Christ, my Lord. As a born-again, new creation in Christ Jesus, I cast out and off any attack on me in Jesus' name! Be gone now and don't come back! It's done, in Jesus' name!"

Then, you thank God, praising the Father, Jesus, and the Holy Spirit, for the salvation and divine health that have been provided to you. You do this with full confidence that God's Word is true.

This lifestyle is not reserved for "super-Christians." It is for *every believer* who dares to believe that God's Word is true!

Chapter 8
What Hinders Healing?

If healing is already ours, why aren't more people healed?

The Bible gives us three main reasons:

1. Unrepentant Sin

Sin separates us from God, clouds our conscience, and hinders our faith. While Jesus paid for all our sins at Calvary, past, present, and future, willful, unrepentant sin blocks us from receiving God's Word and truth. When sin is left unrepentant, it can create a foothold for the enemy in our lives (James 5:15–16). That's why 1 John 1:9 is so vital: be sure you've given all your sins to Jesus and are actively turning away from them.

2. Unforgiveness

Jesus made it clear that we must forgive others, even up to 490 times a day. If we don't forgive others, we ourselves are not forgiven by God (Mark 11:25–26). Unforgiveness is toxic; it poisons your prayer life and damages your relationship with God. It opens the door to the enemy, bringing bitterness and all kinds of wickedness into your life.

3. Unbelief

In His Word, God calls unbelief *evil*. It is the opposite of faith and completely blocks God's power from working in our lives. Doubt and unbelief cancel out faith. In my opinion, this is the greatest hindrance to healing. James 1:6–7 tells us that if we waver in doubt and unbelief, we will receive nothing from the Lord.

Many believers pray for healing, but they don't speak to their mountain, and they don't truly believe that God *wants* them healed. Yet Jesus tells us in Mark 11:24 to pray in faith, *believing*.

Here's the Truth:

God has already said *Yes* to your healing. He wants you healed and has already provided for your healing through Jesus Christ. He is simply waiting for you to agree with His Word.

You don't need *more* faith, you just need to remove unbelief and doubt. Fill your heart with God's Word, His truth. Then speak that truth over every lie of the enemy.

Choose to believe!

Chapter 9
Religion vs Relationship

Too many believers are trapped in religion, bound by religious rules, traditions, rituals, and fear. Religion often portrays God as a distant, all-knowing being who is directly responsible for everything that happens on earth, both good and bad. It adds to Scripture when it supports tradition and ignores or dismisses Scripture when it does not. Religion often embraces beliefs not found in the Bible, while simultaneously rejecting direct commands from God through Jesus Christ that *are* clearly stated in Scripture.

Religion always has an excuse for disobedience to God's Word, saying things like, "That's not for today!" But Jesus didn't come to start a religion; He came to restore our relationship with the Father.

When you walk in relationship with God, you trust the Father's heart. You believe He loves you. You trust Him and take Him at His Word, choosing His truth over your feelings. You stop asking "why?" and start believing and declaring His promises over yourself and others.

Relationship means knowing God, and more importantly, being known by Him. It's hearing Him speak to you through the indwelling Holy Spirit and knowing Him through His Holy Word, the Bible.

This is why religious spirits are so harmful. They won't receive the truth of God's Word for themselves and actively hinder others from receiving it. Religious spirits don't want you healed or walking in anything beyond the natural. They only operate in the natural and always have explanations for why miracles, signs, and wonders no longer happen. But they offer no healing, no miracles, no power, only excuses.

Notice how harshly Jesus rebuked the religious leaders of His day. They knew the Scriptures, but for the sake of their traditions, they ignored the truth and denied the power of God.

John 3:2 says, *"Rabbi, we know that you are a teacher who has come from God. For no one could perform the signs you are doing if God were not with him."*

And Acts 10:38 declares that Jesus came to heal all who were oppressed by the devil.

Religion offers no healing to the oppressed, only justifications for their continued suffering. But when you understand that God loves you, that healing is part of His nature, and that you walk in relationship with Him, healing becomes personal. Walking in divine health becomes natural, as it should be for a child of God!

Chapter 10
Teaching the Next Generation

As I grew in my understanding of healing and walking in divine health, I realized something important: everyone who is Born Again needs this teaching too! I wanted my children to have this knowledge, so I began texting them simple, faith-based steps they could follow to receive healing through God and His Word. These steps weren't just good advice, they were spiritual weapons for warfare.

Here are some of the core principles I shared:

- Recognize sickness as a spiritual attack.

- Never accept symptoms as normal or just a part of life.

- Speak the symptoms out loud.

- Declare God's Word with authority.

- Never confess sickness, illness, or disease; instead, confess healing.

- Thank God for His Word and His blessings of forgiveness and healing.

The enemy would love to keep this truth from you and from the next generation. But God is raising up warriors, those who know who they are in Christ Jesus and understand what our Heavenly Father has provided. They will know their identity, what belongs to them, and how to walk in the authority they have in Christ!

Chapter 11
Practical Declarations and Daily Practices

Walking in Divine Health

Walking in divine health is not complicated. It begins with knowing who you are in Christ Jesus, recognizing what dwells within you, and understanding that no weapon formed against you can prosper. The enemy is a liar. If he can get you to ignore God's Word and His promises, and instead accept his attacks as normal, then he has done his job. Don't allow that to happen.

The Bible teaches us that life and death are in the power of the tongue. What we say, believing we receive, matters. So, read and believe God's Word. Speak what the Word of God says is true, and watch your life transform completely from the inside out!

Below are the text message steps I have sent to friends and family to help them receive healing and stay healed. Please feel free to follow these **Practical Steps to Divine Health**:

To be healed of anything in your body, you need to know these 3 foundational truths:

1. **Sickness and disease come from the enemy, not from God.**

2. **Jesus took all sickness and disease, past, present, and future, upon Himself at Calvary.**

3. God provides instructions for healing through His Word.

If you agree with these three truths, you're ready to continue. If not, I can provide the scriptures that support them so you can study, believe, and come into agreement with these principles.

Next, read and believe these scriptures:

1. **Isaiah 53:4–5**, "By His stripes, we are healed."

This means everyone has access to healing through the stripes Jesus took on His body.

2. **Matthew 8:17**, "He Himself took our infirmities and bore our sicknesses."

Jesus bore all sickness and disease at the Atonement.

3. **1 Peter 2:24,** "By His wounds you were healed."

Healing is a finished work made available to all believers.

Then, believe and apply these powerful truths about your words:

1. **Proverbs 18:21**, *"Life and death are in the power of the tongue."* Our words carry spiritual weight; what we say can bring life or death.

2. **Mark 11:23**, *"Whoever says to this mountain, 'Be removed and cast into the sea,' and does not doubt in his heart, but believes that those things he says will be done, he will have whatever he says."*

This is a Kingdom principle: when you speak God's Word in faith, believing in your heart, it will come to pass.

These truths may seem confusing at first, but they are actually quite simple: it's about believing the words you speak and ensuring those words align with what the Bible says. When your words are in agreement with God's Word, and you believe them in your heart,

God performs His Word in your life.

Next, we need to read and believe:

Mark 5:27–34 depicts a person doing exactly what we've just discussed, acting in faith and receiving healing through belief in Jesus.

Luke 10:19 is true; Jesus has given us, as born-again believers, power and authority over all the power of the enemy. As children of God, we have the right to use the name of Jesus Christ to cast out the devil and resist any attack on our bodies. Because Jesus has already defeated the enemy, he must obey our commands in Jesus' name! This is a powerful truth.

1 Corinthians 6:17 says that we are one spirit with the Lord.

Romans 8:11 confirms that we are born again and that the same Spirit who raised Jesus from the dead now dwells in us. That Spirit gives life to our mortal bodies, our flesh and bones.

We also need to understand:

Your human spirit, your heart, is the new creation that is made alive when you are born again.

Your soul is your intellect, your mind, and your five senses. This part of you is being renewed as you grow in the Word.

Your body is your physical self, your organs, blood, flesh, and bones.

These three parts make up who you are: Spirit, Soul, and Body.

The enemy cannot attack your newly created spirit, your heart. But because your soul is still being renewed and is not made new at salvation, the enemy targets your soul (mind) and your body.

However, you are not defenseless!

The same Spirit that raised Christ from the dead lives in you, and Jesus Christ has given you authority over all the power of the enemy. You can and must use this authority to cast out and resist any attack. You do not have to accept or tolerate these attacks!

This is where many people struggle with healing:

It requires you to watch your words.

Don't speak the symptoms ("I've got this or that").

Instead, speak what the Word of God says and believe it to be true:

"By His stripes, I am completely healed."

Yes, the symptoms may already be present in your body, and yes, you may feel miserable. It's tempting to tell others what you're feeling. But instead, declare God's truth the moment you notice a symptom:

Say this:

"In Jesus' name, I command all sickness, illness, and disease to leave my body now and never come back! I am a child of God, healed and set free by Jesus Christ and His redemptive work at Calvary.

I use the authority given to me by Jesus, and I resist the devil! Leave my body now, in Jesus' name!

I walk in divine health, completely healed from every attack, in the name of Jesus Christ, my Lord and

Savior!"

"Now go from me, you foul spirit of infirmity, and any unclean spirit sent by the enemy! I command you to leave now and never come back, in the mighty name of Jesus Christ!"

Speak directly to your symptoms.

If it's a headache, say:

"In Jesus' name, headache, leave now and don't come back! I am healed and whole by the stripes of Jesus. By His name and through faith in His name, I am completely healed!"

Give thanks:

"Thank You, Jesus! I praise and glorify You for the healing You provided at Calvary. Thank you, God, for making me whole and healed. In Jesus' name, Amen!"

Then trust God. Believe His Word and let Him handle it.

Go on with your day as usual, believing God's Word, not the enemy's lies!

Important Note:

When you first begin to do this, the enemy may try to increase the symptoms to make it seem like it's not working. He does this because he knows what James 1:6–7 says: if you doubt God's Word, he has a legal right to continue afflicting you.

I've experienced this kind of increased attack myself. In the beginning, I had to repeat the declarations above multiple times a day as I began walking in divine health.

Just stay firm. Trust God. Believe His Word. Let him take care of it.

That's really all you need to never be sick again.

As you spend time in the Word, you'll discover even more truth and be able to apply more Scriptures to your life.

It's so important to spend time reading and meditating on the Word, remember the Parable of the Sower. The Bible is the seed, and your heart is the soil. If you want a good harvest, plant good seed!

Speak the Word, not the world.

Remember these truths, and you'll walk in victory. You've got this!

Chapter 12
Scriptures for Healing and Authority

Powerful Bible Verses for Your Walk in Divine Health

Here are some powerful Bible verses to study and meditate on as you walk in divine health:

- **Isaiah 53:5** – By His stripes we are healed.

- **Matthew 8:17** – Jesus took all our sickness and disease upon Himself.

- **1 Peter 2:24** – By His stripes we were healed (It's a completed work!).

- **Mark 11:23-24** – We have what we say, believing.

- **Luke 10:19** – Jesus gave us authority.

- **Psalm 103:3** – He forgives all your sins and heals all your diseases.

- **Mark 2:5-11** – Jesus shows that forgiveness of sins and healing are both completed works.

- **Proverbs 18:21** – Life and death are in the power of the tongue.

- **Mark 5:28** – For she said... and received what she said.

- **Luke 17:21** – The kingdom of God dwells within us.

- **1 Corinthians 6:17** – Our born-again spirit and the Lord are one.

- **Romans 8:11** – The Holy Spirit gives life to our mortal bodies.

- **Acts 3:16** – Faith in the name of Jesus Christ has made this man whole.

- **Acts 10:38** – Jesus went around healing all who were oppressed by the devil.

Chapter 13
Scriptural Methods of Healing

The Bible refers to the gift of healing in 1 Corinthians 12:9 as *the gift of healing*, indicating that there is more than one way to receive healing. Let's take a look at these different methods and uncover the truth found in God's Word:

1. Laying on of Hands

Jesus laid hands on the sick, and He commanded believers to do the same in Mark 16:18.

2. Anointing with Oil and Prayer of Faith

We are instructed in James 5:13-14 to anoint the sick with oil and pray in faith, believing for healing.

3. Holy Communion

In 1 Corinthians 11:29-30, we see the importance of discerning the Lord's body, acknowledging the bread as Jesus' broken body for our healing, and the cup as His blood for the forgiveness of sins.

4. Agreement in Prayer

One of the most powerful ways to receive healing is by standing in agreement with others. Matthew 18:18-20 teaches that when two or more are gathered and agree in prayer, it shall be done.

By believing the Word of God and applying the Word of God, you will see God move mightily on your behalf, because *God watches over His Word to perform it!*

Powerful truth!

Conclusion

This concludes my book, Speaking to the Sickness & Disease. Remember, healing is our birthright as children of God. Jesus provided the healing, so let us honor Him and His Word by walking in that truth. We truly are a sign and a wonder to the unsaved world.

Please feel free to reach out and let me know how you're doing. I'd love to encourage you and support you in fulfilling all the plans and purposes God has for your life.

The Lord bless you and keep you!

In His love,

Scott Jay Daniels

906 Michigan St

Hibbing, MN 55746

Email: sdaniels215@yahoo.com

Phone: (218) 969-8126

www.ingramcontent.com/pod-product-compliance
Lightning Source LLC
Chambersburg PA
CBHW040846010826
48978CB00012BB/915